Big Sister, Little Sister

For my wonderful big sister
G.S.

To my one and only big sister
Hannah and her little Joseph
G.B.

First published 2006 by Macmillan Children's Books
a division of Macmillan Publishers Limited
20 New Wharf Road, London N1 9RR
Basingstoke and Oxford
Associated companies throughout the world
www.panmacmillan.com

ISBN-13: 978-1-4050-0904-1 (HB)
ISBN-10: 1-405-00904-7 (HB)

ISBN-13: 978-1-4050-0905-8 (PB)
ISBN-10: 1-405-00905-5 (PB)

Text copyright © Gillian Shields 2006
Illustrations copyright © Georgie Birkett 2006

1 3 5 7 9 8 6 4 2

A CIP catalogue record for this book
is available for the British Library.

Printed in Belgium by Proost

Big Sister, Little Sister

Gillian Shields ❋ Georgie Birkett

MACMILLAN CHILDREN'S BOOKS

Big sister plays princess,

Little sister
holds her dress.

Big sister points her toe,

Little sister
has a go.

Big sister rides a bike,

Little sister has a trike.

Big sister reads a book,

Little sister
takes a look.

Big sister
plays outside,

Little sister
wants to hide.

Big sister likes to draw,

Little sister
paints the floor.

Big sister swims about,

Little sister splashes out.

Big sister roller-skates,

Little sister
hesitates.

Big sister waves goodbye,

Little sister
starts to cry.

Big sister's
home again,

Little sister's
happy then.

"Big sister, I love you."

"Little one, I love you too!"